UNICORN ACADEMY
...Where magic happens!

Lyra rode Misty into the cave. Misty picked her way cautiously over the rubble, her hooves slipping and sliding. "Follow us, everyone," Lyra said in excitement, "and keep your eyes open for the next piece of the map!"

**UNICORN ACADEMY**
*...Where magic happens!*

# HAVE YOU READ?

Sophia and Rainbow

Scarlett and Blaze

Ava and Star

Isabel and Cloud

Layla and Dancer

Olivia and Snowflake

Rosa and Crystal

Ariana and Whisper

Matilda and Pearl

Freya and Honey

Violet and Twinkle

Isla and Buttercup

Lily and Feather

Phoebe and Shimmer

Zara and Moonbeam

Aisha and Silver

# LOOK OUT FOR:

Evie and Sunshine

# Lyra and Misty

**Julie Sykes**

illustrated by
**Lucy Truman**

nosy crow

To Elsie. May all your dreams sparkle
and take you to the stars!

First published in the UK in 2021 by Nosy Crow Ltd
The Crow's Nest, 14 Baden Place
Crosby Row, London, SE1 1YW

www.nosycrow.com

ISBN: 978 1 78800 949 2

Nosy Crow and associated logos are trademarks
and/or registered trademarks of Nosy Crow Ltd.

Text copyright © Julie Sykes and Linda Chapman, 2021
Illustrations copyright © Lucy Truman, 2021
Cover typography © Joel Holland, 2021

A CIP catalogue record for this book is available from the British Library.

Printed and bound in Great Britain by Clays Ltd, Elcograf S.p.A.

Papers used by Nosy Crow are made from
wood grown in sustainable forests.

MIX
Paper from
responsible sources
FSC® C018072

1 3 5 7 9 10 8 6 4 2

# CHAPTER ONE

It was a frosty afternoon and the new students at Unicorn Academy were chatting and laughing as they groomed their unicorns. Lyra pushed her long light-brown hair behind her ears and put down her brush. "Now for your hooves," she said to her unicorn, Misty. "Would you like gold, purple or pink hoof polish?"

Misty had been staring into the distance, lost in thought. She blinked. "Oh … um … I don't mind," she said, nuzzling Lyra. "You choose. I'm not very good at making decisions."

"Well, I love making decisions, so we're a perfect

match!" Lyra said, putting her arms round Misty
and breathing in her sweet unicorn smell. "Let's
use gold!"

Misty was a very pretty snow-white unicorn
patterned with swirls of purple and spring green.
Lyra had been thrilled when, the day before,

Ms Nettles, the academy's strict headteacher, had put them together in the Pairing Ceremony.

Lyra picked up the tub of sparkly gold hoof polish and a brush. "I still can't believe I'm actually here at Unicorn Academy," she said happily.

She glanced around her; the academy stable block was clean and shiny, with stalls for the unicorns on either side of the wide aisles. Automated trollies ran up and down carrying bales of straw and buckets of sky berries, the unicorns' favourite food, while the drinking water came from silver troughs that magically filled with multicoloured water from Sparkle Lake.

Lyra had wanted to go to the academy for as long as she could remember. Her cousin, Scarlett, had also been a student a few years ago and she had told Lyra all about the amazing adventures she'd had with her friends and their unicorns.

*I am* definitely *going to have adventures while I'm*

*here*, Lyra thought, as she painted Misty's hooves.

Misty gave Lyra a look from under her long eyelashes. "Are … are you missing your family at all, Lyra?"

Lyra considered it. She had thought she would miss her parents and sister loads but there had been so much going on from the moment she'd arrived at the academy that she hadn't missed home much at all. "No, not really," she admitted.

Misty hung her head and Lyra wondered if Misty was homesick. She decided it was best to distract her by talking about something different. "I wonder what magical power you'll have," she said, "and when you'll discover it. It'll be so cool to be able to do magic!"

Before they could graduate and become guardians of Unicorn Island, students had to bond with their unicorn and each unicorn had to discover their magical power. Sometimes students

and their unicorns needed more than one year to complete everything and had to return for a second.

"I really hope you have the power to do something super exciting, like being able to fly or turn invisible," Lyra went on. "Those powers would be awesome!" She glanced across the aisle to where Sienna, one of the girls she shared Ruby dorm with, was plaiting her unicorn's mane with blue and purple ribbons. "Hey, Sienna, if Sparkle could have any magical power, what would you choose?" she called.

Sienna was tall with corkscrew curls that reached her shoulders. Her brown eyes lit up as she considered the question. "I'd choose for Sparkle to be able to gallop at the speed of light so we could beat everyone every time we raced!"

Sparkle, a very athletic unicorn, stamped his hoof. "That would be fun!"

Sienna's words gave Lyra an idea. "Why don't we go and have some races? Or, better still, go exploring. Ivy? Evie?" she shouted to the other two girls in their dorm. "What do you think? Shall we go for a Ruby dorm ride?"

Evie was carrying a bucket of water towards her unicorn, Sunshine. She looked round as Lyra called her name and promptly tripped over her feet. She cried out as she fell, dropping the bucket and sending water splashing everywhere.

"Evie! Are you OK?" cried Ivy.

"I'm fine," said Evie, blushing bright red as they all dashed over and helped her up. "I'm so

clumsy," she groaned. "Look at this mess." She tried to grab a nearby broom to sweep the water away but her fingers fumbled with the handle and the broom fell into Sienna. She gasped. "Oh no! Sorry!"

"No problem," said Sienna with a grin. "But maybe I'll do the sweeping up!"

"Yes, you should go and get some dry clothes," said Ivy to Evie. "You're soaked through."

"And when you come back, we can all go exploring!" Lyra said eagerly. "There are so many places we haven't been yet – the maze, the cross-country course, the woods—"

"What about the safari trail? I want to see that," interrupted Ivy. "There are supposed to be some really interesting animals there."

"I've heard there are some incredible creatures in the woods," said Lyra. She'd also heard the woods were dangerous and the thought of checking them out made excitement fizz through her.

"Aren't they out of bounds?" asked Sienna.

"It doesn't stop us from going to the edge of them and having a look, though, does it?" said Lyra with a grin. "I definitely think it's time for Ruby dorm to go exploring!"

# CHAPTER TWO

A little while later, the four girls trotted their unicorns away from the stable block. The air was frosty and the grass crunched under the unicorns' hooves as they skirted round the edge of Sparkle Lake.

Sparkle Lake's water had magical properties. It sprang up from the centre of the earth, cascaded through an ornate fountain in the middle of the lake and then flowed away around the island. The water helped all the people, plants and animals on the island flourish and it also strengthened the unicorns' magic.

Lyra grinned as they left the lake and headed towards the lush green meadows. Here she was, with her own unicorn, out on an adventure at last! She loved exploring. When she was older, she wanted to be an archaeologist who discovered unknown places and found precious artefacts. She couldn't think of a more fun job!

"So, where are we going to go?" Sienna asked her.

"The woods," said Lyra instantly.

"Are you sure, Lyra?" said Misty. "They sound dangerous and we shouldn't go in if they're out of bounds."

"We'll stay on the edge. It'll be fun," said Lyra. "That's if we can find them, of course!"

"You mean we might get lost?" asked Misty anxiously.

Lyra ruffled her mane. "Yep! That's the best thing about exploring – you never know what's

going to happen!"

"Oh," said Misty, gulping.

"Come on, I'm bored of trotting. Let's canter," said Sienna. "Or, even better, gallop!"

Sienna urged Sparkle on and they all raced across the grounds and into the meadow. A sparkling multicoloured stream wound through the long grass and the unicorns stopped beside it to have a refreshing drink.

"Let's have a contest to see who can jump the widest part of the stream," said Sienna, her eyes glinting.

"Yes!" agreed Sparkle, playfully splashing Flame, who was drinking next to him. "You're pretty fast, Flame, but I bet I can jump further than you."

"But I was really looking forward to going to the woods," said Lyra, disappointed.

"I think we should do what the others want,

Lyra," said Misty quickly. "Jumping the stream sounds fun!"

Lyra sighed. "OK."

"Great! I'll start," called Sienna. She and Sparkle galloped towards the stream and soared over it. "Beat that, Lyra!" Sienna said, laughing over her shoulder.

Lyra forgot her frustration. "You're on! Come on, Misty!"

Misty set off towards an even wider part of the stream. Lyra gripped her long mane and felt her heart leap as Misty took off. The fast-flowing water sparkled beneath them for a brief second and then they landed safely on the far bank.

"Our go!" called Ivy, and Flame leapt gracefully over the water.

But Evie shook her head when it was her and Sunshine's turn. "We'll just watch." She clapped and cheered as the other three took it in turns to

jump wider and wider stretches.

It was a close competition. Ivy and Flame dropped out first and then, when Sienna and Sparkle had jumped a really wide part of the stream, Misty shook her head. "I can't jump that far," she told Lyra. "I'm sure of it."

"OK," said Lyra, not wanting to force her. "That's fine. You win," she called to Sienna. "Well done," she added generously. "Sparkle was great."

Sienna whooped in delight. "We're the champions!" she said, punching the air. She leant down and hugged Sparkle. He snorted happily and then jumped back over the stream to join the others.

"We should probably go back to the stables," said Evie, looking at the sun sinking in the sky.

"Yes, it'll be dark soon," said Sienna. "Come on. Last one there is a snot-flop snail!" She clapped her heels to Sparkle's sides.

Laughing and shouting, the girls galloped after her.

After settling the unicorns with big buckets of sky berries and bulging haynets, Lyra and the others walked back to school. The sun was setting and the academy's tall marble and glass towers glowed against the red-gold sky. Lyra's eyes sought out the tower where their dormitory was situated. Ruby dorm was on the top floor of the north tower, along with Topaz dorm. The setting sun made the five windows flame pink.

Lyra frowned and stopped for a moment, letting the others walk on. Five! That wasn't right, was it? The two dorms were identical and they had two windows each, so why was there a fifth window above Ruby dorm?

*There must be another room – a hidden room – above our dorm*, she realised.

"Hey!" she called.

The others looked round.

"What's up?" asked Ivy.

"Look at our tower and count the number of windows."

They all glanced up at the tower and then turned back to Lyra with puzzled expressions.

"There are five," said Sienna. "So?"

Lyra quickly explained what she'd discovered. "There must be a hidden room! I'm going to try to find it. Ruby dorm, there's a mystery we need to solve…"

# CHAPTER THREE

The girls stood on the circular landing at the top of the tower with puzzled expressions on their faces. "If there is a secret room, there's absolutely no way up to it from here," said Sienna.

On one side was their dorm – Ruby – and on the other side was Topaz dorm where four boys, Sam, Reuben, Archie and Nawaz, slept.

"There isn't a hidden door anywhere out here," said Lyra, tapping the wall between the dorms.

"And we've checked our room," said Ivy. "We

didn't find any hidden doors in there."

"What about in the boys' dorm?" suggested Sienna.

"We should probably ask them before we go and look," said Evie slowly.

"If we don't touch anything of theirs, I'm sure it'll be OK," said Sienna.

Lyra nodded. "We can't give up yet. First rule of exploring. You have to take risks!" Turning the door handle, she went inside.

The boys' room was a mirror image of the girls', but decorated in blue and gold rather than red. There were four beds, each with a blue-and-gold-coloured duvet. There was a fluffy gold rug on the floor and blue-and-gold curtains at the windows. On the chest of drawers beside each bed, a lamp glowed with a golden light. Next to their lamp, each boy had put photos of their family and pets, and they each had a shelf for their books,

magazines and school folders.

Lyra's nose wrinkled at the lingering smell of sweaty feet as she picked her way across the floor. A tapestry of three unicorn foals hung on the wall. Could there be a door hidden behind it? She pushed it aside. No, there was just solid wall. The girls checked every centimetre of the room but found nothing.

"There's no entrance here either," said Lyra in frustration. She really wanted to solve the mystery!

"Time to give up," said Ivy, going to the door. "I vote we go and make a hot chocolate in our lounge."

"We can't just abandon the search!" protested Lyra.

"I vote for hot chocolate too," said Sienna.

"With marshmallows," agreed Evie.

Lyra gave in and led the way down the spiral staircase. At the bottom of the staircase were

two lounges, one for Topaz dorm and one for Ruby dorm. On the wall between them was a large tapestry of a magnificent unicorn with a golden mane standing beside a forest pool. A tear trickled down the unicorn's face. Her name was embroidered at the bottom: *Daybreak*. The strange tapestry had caught Lyra's attention on their first day at the school, making her

wonder who Daybreak was and why she was crying. She looked at it as she waited for Ivy and Evie to catch up. Evie had almost reached the bottom when she missed a step. She clattered down the last three stairs and landed on her bottom.

"Evie! Are you OK?" Lyra rushed to help her up.

"I'm fine." Evie turned bright red as Lyra helped her to her feet.

Lyra glanced down and noticed a tiny carving scratched into the stone on the rise of the bottom step. "It's Daybreak!" she said in surprise. "That unicorn on the tapestry over there. It's definitely her. Look at the teardrop on her face and the pool of water at her feet. But why would someone put it here?"

There was a circle round the picture and Lyra ran a finger over it. To her astonishment the circle depressed slightly. She pressed harder. "It's a button!" she cried.

With a grating sound, a section of the wall behind the tapestry slid back.

Sienna and Ivy squealed and raced over. Pulling aside the tapestry they saw a second spiral

staircase, smaller and darker than the one they had just come down.

"Look at that!" said Sienna in surprise.

"I knew it." Lyra could hardly breathe with excitement. "It has to be the way up to the secret room! Come on, let's check it out."

Cobwebs festooned the staircase like bunting and the steps were covered in a thick layer of dust. "No one's been up here in ages," Lyra commented as she climbed.

At the top they reached a small room with a window set in the curved wall. The stone walls and the dark wooden floorboards were bare and the window was grimy.

Lyra stared around the gloomy room. It was really weird to think she was standing above Ruby dorm in a space that looked like it had been forgotten about for years.

"There's nothing in here," said Sienna

disappointedly. "Why bother to hide a room and not put anything exciting in it?"

She and Ivy went to the window and looked out while Evie hovered anxiously in the doorway.

Lyra walked around the room, looking carefully. When a floorboard under her foot gave way slightly, she jumped back, thinking the wood must be rotten. She peered down at it. The floorboard looked fine, so she knelt to investigate. One end of the board dipped below the level of the others. Then her sharp eyes caught sight of something strange. At the other end of the floorboard was a hinge. She almost hadn't seen it because it was made of dark metal and blended in with the wood.

"Can we go back down now?" asked Evie uneasily. "We might get into trouble."

"Wait!" said Lyra, pulling a penknife from her pocket. It had lots of useful tools in it including

a screwdriver. She wriggled the flat end of the screwdriver under the end of the floorboard and levered it up, revealing a cavity.

Lyra's heart beat fast. She lay down and reached into the space.

"What are you doing?" asked Sienna, coming over.

Lyra's fingers closed on a piece of paper, and she gasped. "I've found something!" she said, pulling it out.

The other three crowded round.

"What is it?" Ivy asked eagerly.

Sitting back up, Lyra smoothed the rectangle of paper out. It was thick and sepia-coloured, the edges curling with age. There were pictures drawn in each corner in faded ink and in the centre was some writing in an old-fashioned curly script.

"It's just some scrap paper," said Sienna, disappointed.

"But why would someone hide an old scrap of paper?" asked Evie.

Sienna shrugged. "It probably just fell under the floorboard and—"

"No, wait!" Lyra looked up, her eyes alight with excitement. "I think it's a treasure map!"

# CHAPTER FOUR

"A treasure map?" breathed Sienna. "For real?"

"Yes! Look!" Lyra pointed to the top right-hand corner. "That's a picture of the school with Sparkle Lake and here –" she pointed to the bottom left-hand corner – "is a tower."

"And the bit in that corner," added Evie, "looks like a maze. That mark right at the very edge could be part of an X!"

Sienna gasped. "X marks the spot! Oh, wow! It really could be a treasure map!"

"What does the writing say, Lyra?" asked Evie eagerly.

Lyra screwed up her eyes. The letters were really faint and the handwriting was hard to read. There were four lines. "It's just a list of random things." She read them out. "*The Northernmost Door, The Phoenix's Claw, The Salamander's Stare, The Dragon's Lair.*"

"What does it all mean?" breathed Sienna.

"I've no idea, but I'm sure if we can work them out, we'll find the treasure – whatever it is!" Lyra's eyes were wide with excitement.

"Wait." Evie took the paper from Lyra and examined it carefully. "I think this is just one *part* of a treasure map. Look, these two outside edges are very old and curled but these two edges are much sharper, almost as though they were cut by scissors. The picture of the school isn't a complete picture; it's been cut in half. The tower and maze too. I think this is just a quarter of the map."

"So where's the rest?" said Sienna.

"Maybe there's more in the hole," said Ivy.

Lyra lay down on her tummy again and felt around, but there wasn't anything else under the floorboards. "No, nothing there," she said. But as she sat up she caught sight of the underside of the piece of paper in Evie's hands.

29

"There's more writing on the other side!" she exclaimed.

Evie turned the map over. "This writing is newer; it's not so faded. Listen!

*Go to the woods for what you seek,*

*Find Daybreak, move stone, follow river deep.*

*Where spiders live and a cave answers your call,*

*The piece lies behind a glittering wall."*

"It's a riddle," said Ivy.

"It's not just a riddle," said Lyra, taking the piece of the map from her. "It's a clue! A clue that will lead us to another part."

"But why would someone cut a map up and hide the bits separately?" wondered Evie.

"I have no idea," said Lyra. Her eyes shone with determination. "But this is a mystery we are going to solve."

Just then, there was the sound of a distant gong ringing.

"It's dinner time!" said Sienna. "We'd better get a move on. We don't want to miss it."

"Definitely not!" agreed Lyra. After dinner a famous archaeologist called Dr Briar was going to be giving a talk to the students. Lyra couldn't wait.

They hurried back down the staircase and out from behind the tapestry. Lyra had just pressed the button to close the secret entrance when the four boys from Topaz dorm came clattering down the stairs.

"What have you been doing?" said Sam, who was tall and thin with wavy blond hair. He looked down his nose at Lyra.

"Have you been having a dust bath?" said Archie with a grin.

"Or cuddling spiders? You've all got cobwebs in your hair," said Reuben.

Lyra shrugged. "We've just been messing

around," she said vaguely.

"How about you?" asked Sienna, quickly changing the subject. "What have you been up to?"

"We've been practising crossnet all afternoon," said Archie as they set off to the refectory together. "We're definitely going to win the inter-dorm tournament tomorrow." Crossnet was a game played on unicorns. Each player had a stick with a net on and they had to pass a ball from player to player, scoring points by throwing the ball through the goal at the end of the pitch. It was fast and furious and lots of fun!

"Boys are the best," chanted Nawaz.

"In your dreams!" Sienna said scornfully. "We'll beat you hands down tomorrow."

"I don't think so—" said Reuben.

"What's that?" Sam interrupted, pointing to the piece of the map that Lyra was holding.

"Nothing," she said quickly. "Just a bit of paper I picked up."

"It looks really old," said Sam, stepping closer.

"Yeah, well, I'm into history and old stuff," said Lyra, stuffing it into her pocket.

"You should show it to my aunt; she might be able to tell you more about it," said Sam.

"Your aunt?"

"Don't you know? My aunt is Dr Angelica Briar, the archaeologist who's giving the talk after dinner."

"Your aunt is Dr Briar?!" Lyra exclaimed.

"Yes." Sam was almost bursting with smugness.

"I've helped her on digs before and I'll be assisting with her talk tonight."

Lyra felt a flash of jealousy. "Oh."

They soon reached the refectory, a long room with windows overlooking the lake. It was lit by hundreds of tiny white lights that sparkled prettily against the dark sky.

"Enjoy the talk," Sam said to Lyra. "If you're very lucky, my aunt might even give you her autograph." He grinned in an annoyingly superior way and walked off.

Lyra scowled after him and then spotted an elegant woman with neat shoulder-length dark hair, who was sitting at the top table with the teachers. Her hair was held back with a diamanté clip and she had rings on all her fingers. She was talking to Ms Nettles, the headteacher. *Dr Briar!* Lyra thought with a lurch of excitement as she recognised her from magazine articles she had read.

"Hey, do you think Sam's right? Shall we show Dr Briar the piece of the map after the talk?" she whispered, nudging the others.

"Good plan," said Ivy.

Sienna and Evie nodded.

Lyra crossed her fingers. Would Dr Briar be able to decipher the words on the map? She really hoped so!

Dinner was delicious – veggie burgers with sweet potato fries and salad followed by gooey chocolate brownies and ice cream. When it was over, the top table was cleared and Sam helped Dr Briar lay out ancient artefacts. Lyra felt a pang of envy as she watched.

"Why are they wearing funny gloves?" asked Ivy, peering over Lyra's shoulder.

"Because the oils in your hand can damage anything old," Lyra explained.

"I hope this talk isn't going to be boring,"

muttered Sienna.

"It won't be!" said Lyra.

She was right. When Dr Briar began her talk, it quickly became clear that she had a wonderful way of bringing history alive, telling the students fascinating stories of how people had once lived and how they had used the objects. To Lyra's surprise Sam chimed in at times and seemed just as enthusiastic as his aunt. He seemed to be genuinely into history and archaeology. He brought round some of the ancient pots, tools and jewellery for everyone to examine.

At the end of the lecture, as the students left, Ruby dorm hung back.

Dr Briar smiled encouragingly at them. "Hello, girls. Is there something you wanted to ask me?"

Shyly Lyra took the map out of her pocket. "We found this earlier. It's got writing and pictures on. We wondered if you might know what they mean."

# Lyra and Misty

Dr Briar smiled. "Let's have a look. Maybe you've stumbled on some great find." Her eyes twinkled.

Lyra blushed as she handed the map over. What if they were wrong and it was just a bit of scrap paper after all?

Dr Briar studied it carefully, her smile changing to a frown of concentration as she turned it this way and that. Lyra held her breath. Dr Briar's eyes were intent. Surely that had to be a good sign?

At last Dr Briar looked up at them. "Well, it's rather fun," she said lightly. "One of my friends who collects old manuscripts would probably love to see it, but I'm sorry to say that it's not of any value."

"Oh!" said Sienna. "So it's not part of a treasure map?"

"A treasure map?" Dr Briar gave a tinkling laugh. "Oh, no, girls. It's clearly old but it's just some random scribblings."

Lyra felt confused. She'd seen how carefully Dr Briar had studied the map. If it was worthless, why had she examined it for so long?

"Where did you find it?" Dr Briar asked curiously.

"In a—" Sienna began.

Lyra wasn't sure why but she suddenly felt that she didn't want to tell Dr Briar about the secret room. "In a room somewhere in school," she finished.

"Well, like I say, I'm sure one of my friends who collects old manuscripts would like to have it, just for the curiosity value," said Dr Briar. "I'll pass it on if you like."

"No," said Lyra quickly, grabbing the paper before Dr Briar could pocket it. "I want to keep it."

Dr Briar's mouth tightened a fraction. "Are you sure?" She increased her grip on the paper.

"Yes, definitely," said Lyra. "I like old things." She watched Dr Briar's face. "That's not a problem, is it? You said it's not valuable."

"Absolutely not." Dr Briar smiled as she let the paper go. "If you change your mind, then just ask Sam to let me know. Which dorm are you, by the way?"

"Ruby," said Evie.

"Great, well, lovely meeting you, girls. I'd better finish up here. If you see Sam, could you ask him to come and have a quick word with me?" Then Dr Briar turned away.

Lyra felt disappointed and confused as they left the hall. She'd seen the interest in Dr Briar's eyes as she had examined the map so it had been a surprise when she'd said it wasn't of any value. An uneasy thought flickered across Lyra's mind. Had Dr Briar been lying? But what possible reason could she have for misleading them?

*Whatever she says, I'm sure it's part of a treasure map,* thought Lyra.

Feeling very glad that she'd managed to hang on to it, she followed the others out of the hall.

# CHAPTER FIVE

The next day, the inter-dorm crossnet tournament was planned for the afternoon, but first Ruby and Topaz dorms had a Geography and Culture lesson. Lyra's dreams had been full of treasure maps and mysterious clues and, while Ms Rivers talked about ecosystems, Lyra thought about the riddle on the back of the map. She recited the words in her head.

*Go to the woods for what you seek,*
*Find Daybreak, move stone, follow river deep.*
*Where spiders live and a cave answers your call,*
*The piece lies behind a glittering wall.*

She frowned. What did it all mean?

"Lyra?"

Lyra jumped as she realised Ms Rivers and the whole class were staring at her.

"S-sorry," she stuttered. "Can you repeat the question?"

Sam sniggered but Ivy sent her a sympathetic smile.

Ms Rivers sighed. "The ecosystem in the woods, can you give me an example of an animal that lives there?"

Across the room, behind Ms Rivers, Evie flapped her arms.

"Birds," said Lyra.

Ms Rivers looked unimpressed. "Yes, Lyra, there are birds in the woods. I was hoping you might name one?"

"Um…"

Evie pulled at her nose and then waggled her

fingers like spiders.

"The stretchy-nosed spidery bird?" guessed Lyra.

Ms Rivers' eyebrows almost hit her hairline as the rest of the class giggled.

"Miss, I think Lyra is talking about the long-beaked spider crow," Sam called out smugly.

"Thank you, Sam," said Ms Rivers. "You are quite correct. Long-beaked spider crows roost near the Echo Caves at the edge of the woods and feed on cave spiders." She glared at Lyra. "Please pay more attention, Lyra."

Lyra blushed and sank down in her seat.

"Who can name any animals that live in the caves?" Ms Rivers asked.

As she moved on, choosing people to answer, something in Lyra's brain clicked and she only just managed to stop herself from gasping out loud. *Cave spiders! Echo Caves!* The words of the riddle ran through her head again: *Where spiders live and a cave answers your call...* An echo was like a voice that sent your words back to you – you could say it answered your call – and there were spiders in the Echo Caves. Maybe the map was hidden in the Echo Caves!

She glanced over at Ivy, Sienna and Evie, her secret swelling inside her and threatening to burst out. But as Ms Rivers' sharp eyes turned on her, she forced herself to pay attention and listen.

At the end of the lesson, Lyra hurried everyone up to their dorm. Shutting the door firmly behind her, she faced her friends.

"I've done it! I've solved the clue. We need to

go to the Echo Caves!" She raced through her explanation.

"I bet you're right," said Evie in excitement. "How about we go there this afternoon?"

"But what about the crossnet tournament?" protested Sienna.

Lyra bit her lip. She wanted to play in the tournament but following the clue was definitely more important. "We can miss it. The teachers said it wasn't compulsory."

"But I want to take part," said Sienna, frowning.

"More than you want to find treasure?" asked Lyra.

Sienna hesitated. "OK, no, I guess I'd rather find another part of the map."

Lyra grinned. "Great! So this afternoon let's go map hunting!"

After lunch, they went to the stables and told the

unicorns their plan. Lyra had a small rucksack with her – it was her explorer's bag. It had things that might come in useful like string, a penknife, a first-aid kit, torches, some snacks and a few spare clothes. *Be adventure-ready*. That was her motto.

She had memorised a map of the school grounds and she and Misty led the way out through the meadow. They followed the stream for a while and then veered off to the left and

headed up a steep hill. At the top, the unicorns stopped and they all looked down at the dark woods spread out on the slopes beneath them, the trees tall and forbidding like stern, watchful guards.

"You know we're not allowed in those woods," said Misty uneasily.

"We don't have to go properly in," said Lyra. "The caves are very near the edge."

They rode down the hill, the unicorns' hooves slipping on loose rocks as they descended. Through the trees they could just make out the caves. One was much larger than the rest and a thick curtain of vines hung down over its gaping mouth.

Misty stopped suddenly. Lyra patted her neck, encouraging her to go on, but she didn't move.

"What's up?" Lyra could barely hide her impatience.

"I heard a noise." Nervously Misty looked around, then snorted and jumped backwards. "Up there! There's something watching from that tree!"

Goosebumps shivered up Lyra's arms and she gripped Misty's mane tightly. Something with a sharp hooked nose peered down at them from between the branches. Lyra tried to tell the others but her mouth was too dry to speak. Sienna and Sparkle rode on, Sparkle's hooves crunching as he stepped on a stick.

There was a startled squawk and a whoosh of air. A huge bird flew out of the tree, its blue-black wings flapping frantically as it soared away. Lyra burst out laughing. "It was only a bird, Misty! A long-beaked spider crow! That means we're definitely in the right place."

By now Sienna and Sparkle had reached the curtain of vines. Sienna pulled it back. "Shall

I lead the way?" she said, peering into the darkness.

*No!* thought Lyra. She wanted to go first!

But it was too late. Sienna and Sparkle were already entering the cave. The others followed. Only Misty remained outside.

"What are you doing, Misty?" said Lyra impatiently. "We need to catch up with the others!"

"I don't want to go in," said Misty. "It could be dangerous!"

"What can you see?" Lyra called to her friends.

"It's empty." Sienna's voice echoed back at her. "But there's a tunnel at the back."

"The next piece of the map might be hidden in the tunnel," said Ivy, her voice echoing too.

Lyra dismounted. She simply had to see this for herself. "Wait up! Don't go any further without me!"

Misty stamped her hoof on the ground as Lyra started towards the cave. "Lyra, come back!"

For a second Lyra caught sight of something sparkling in the air – but then it was gone. A smell wafted past, sweet like candyfloss. It reminded her of something but there wasn't time to think about it. She wanted to see the tunnel! "It'll be fine, Misty – please."

"I don't want to," said Misty.

Lyra gave up trying to persuade her. So instead she pulled her torch out and walked into the cave. The beam picked out the cobwebs hanging from the roof. Large friendly cave spiders with googly eyes and fluffy legs watched the girls curiously. Lyra headed for the tunnel where her friends were standing with their unicorns. There was

a pile of dirt and stones at the entrance.

"It looks like part of the roof's come down," said Evie.

"We can still get through, though." Lyra scrambled over the heap of rubble. "The tunnel clears when you get past this bit. It's wide enough for us to ride through." She turned. "Come on!" she called to Misty.

"Yes, don't be a spoilsport, Misty," said Sienna. "Come and join us."

Flame, Ivy's unicorn, stamped a hoof. "Don't you want to have an adventure?"

"No," Misty called back firmly.

Lyra's torch beam fell on a small picture carved into the stone wall of the tunnel. "There's a tiny unicorn carved into the rock. It has a teardrop on its face. It's Daybreak!"

Lyra's eyes glowed. "Oh, wow. This must mean we have to go down the tunnel. The clue said *Find Daybreak*. Remember?"

The others nodded.

"I'm going on. Who's with me?" asked Lyra.

"Me!" cried everyone except Misty.

"Misty?" Lyra pleaded, scrambling back over the rubble.

"I suppose," Misty muttered.

Lyra was very relieved. She didn't want to have an argument with Misty in front of everyone but there was no way she could turn away from the tunnel now. She ran back to Misty and, vaulting on her back, she rode her into the cave. Misty picked her way cautiously over the rubble, her hooves slipping and sliding. "Follow us, everyone," Lyra said in excitement, "and keep your eyes open for the next piece of the map!"

# CHAPTER SIX

The tunnel sloped downwards. Mosses and lichen clung to the craggy walls and the unicorns' hooves clattered on the stony floor. After they had been riding for some time, the ground levelled out. Several other tunnels joined theirs but at every junction they came to there was a little stone carving of Daybreak showing them which way to go. Lyra could hardly contain her excitement. Were they really about to find another piece of the treasure map?

"Is that water?" asked Sienna as they heard a tinkly sound in the distance.

"It can't be; we're underground," said Ivy.

"Rivers and streams often run underground," said Evie as they rode on.

"Oh, wow!" Lyra breathed as they rounded another corner and the tunnel opened into a vast cavern. Its high ceiling arched above them and a

glittering rainbow-coloured river flowed through it. The rocky walls glowed softly with a strange shimmering light. Gold-striped fish leapt in and out of the water while huge dragonflies with green iridescent wings darted above them.

"Which way do we go?" said Ivy, looking up and down the river.

"Here's another picture," Sienna said excitedly, as she stretched down from Sparkle's back to point at a boulder to the right. Sure enough, the boulder was marked with a tiny Daybreak.

They rode beside the river, following the carvings until a sheer wall of rock rose up in front of them and the river disappeared into a narrow hole to continue its underground path. There was no way they could follow it. To their right were two tunnels.

"Which one should we take?" Lyra shone her torch into each of them, looking for another tiny

picture of a unicorn, but she couldn't find one anywhere.

"That tunnel looks bigger. I bet it's this way," cried Sienna, riding past Lyra and Misty.

Evie and Sunshine and Ivy and Flame followed her. Lyra felt a flicker of annoyance. This was her expedition, not Sienna's! "Hurry up, we're getting left behind," she said to Misty, who was stepping very cautiously over the uneven floor.

The tunnel twisted and turned until they saw a circle of light ahead.

"That must be the way out," said Evie.

"But we still haven't found the map," protested Lyra.

The others seemed more interested in seeing where they were going to come out.

"I bet we're in the mountains," said Sienna.

"Or we've walked a circle and we're back in the woods," said Evie.

Lyra switched off her torch as they emerged, blinking, into the daylight. There was an old brick shed in front of them with a compost heap and a willow tree beside it.

"Where are we?" asked Sienna, looking around.

"We're in the vegetable garden," said Lyra as she rode Misty round the shed and saw the school gardens spread out in front of her.

"Look," whispered Evie, who had followed her. "Sam and Flash are over there. It looks like they're cooling off after the crossnet tournament."

"I wonder which dorm won," said Sienna. "I hope it wasn't Topaz or we'll never hear the end of it."

"Don't let Sam see us," said Lyra. "He'll only want to know what we've been doing."

They ducked back behind the dilapidated shed and waited for Sam and Flash to leave before they headed back to the stables. On their way they saw

a group of students from Sapphire dorm clustered round a dainty unicorn with a bright orange and gold mane.

"What's going on?" said Ivy curiously.

Lexi and Katy, two of the girls in Sapphire dorm, saw them and waved. "Come and watch!" Lexi called. "Elise and Peony have just discovered Peony's magic. They're first in the year."

"What can Peony do?" Lyra asked eagerly.

Elise, a tall girl with curly red hair, beamed. "She's got summoning magic." She put her hand on her unicorn's neck. "Peony, please will you get my hoodie from the stables?"

Peony stamped a hoof, blue sparkles flew up and a sweet smell of burnt sugar filled the air. A few seconds later, a blue hoodie came flying towards them. It hit Peony's head and she snorted in surprise as it caught on her ears and dangled from them.

# Lyra and Misty

Elise giggled. "We've still got some practising to do, but isn't it amazing?" She hugged Peony who nuzzled her.

"It's awesome!" said Lyra, very pleased for Elise and Peony, but also feeling a flash of jealousy. Elise was so lucky! When would Misty discover her magic?

"How did you find it out?" said Sienna, who also looked a bit envious.

"It was when we were playing crossnet," said Elise. "The ball just kept flying out of other people's nets into mine!"

"We were about to win the match twenty goals to one," said Lexi, "but then Ms Nettles realised what was going on and she gave the match to

Topaz dorm."

"Who won the tournament overall?" asked Ivy.

"Topaz," said Katy.

Sienna groaned.

Elise gave them a curious look. "Where were you lot?"

"We had something else to do," Lyra said vaguely.

Katy grinned. "The Topaz boys said you were scared they'd beat you!"

"As if!" said Sienna. "I can't believe it," she went on grumpily as they rode away. "Now the boys think we were too chicken to play against them. If we'd been playing crossnet, we might have won the tournament and maybe one of our unicorns would have discovered *their* magic. Instead we just got to ride down lots of tunnels and found nothing at all."

"We must have taken a wrong turning somewhere," said Lyra. "We should go back and try again. There's just enough time before dinner…"

The others shook their heads.

"No, not now. The unicorns are tired," said Evie.

"And I'm hungry," said Ivy.

"But—" Lyra began.

"Chill!" Ivy interrupted. "Wherever the map is hidden, it's safe, Lyra."

Sienna nodded. "Ivy's right. We can have another go at finding it tomorrow or at the weekend."

Lyra sighed. She knew the others were right but she wanted to find the map *now*!

# CHAPTER SEVEN

Back in the stables, Lyra brushed Misty down and fetched her some sky berries. "I wish we'd found another piece of the map," she said.

"Mmm," said Misty. She gave a shiver. "I didn't like those caves much."

"They were fine," said Lyra. "There wasn't anything to be scared of."

Misty sighed. "When I was little I found everything scary. My older sister, Dewdrop, used to tease me and say I was scared of my own shadow. She's always been much braver than me." She snorted sadly. "I do miss her. I bet you'd

like her, Lyra. She's—"

"Hey," Lyra interrupted. She didn't want Misty to start feeling sad about missing her family. "I've just had an idea. Maybe I can persuade the others to go back to the caves tomorrow morning? Ms Rivers has organised a treasure hunt. It's supposed to help us learn more about the school and the grounds but I bet we could sneak off and no one would notice. What do you think?"

"You could try," Misty muttered.

"I will!" said Lyra. "A treasure hunt is fun but finding another piece of a real treasure map will be even better! See you later, Misty."

She left the stable block and caught up with her friends as they reached the school building. "How about this for a plan?" Lyra said as they went up the staircase to Ruby dorm. "Instead of doing the treasure hunt tomorrow, we—" She broke off with a gasp as Sienna opened the door to their dorm.

Their room had been completely ransacked! Clothes spilled from open drawers and the floor was strewn with books, pencils and papers.

"What's happened?" asked Evie, her eyes huge.

Lyra and the others picked their way through the mess to their beds.

"None of my things are missing," said Lyra in relief.

"Nor mine," said Ivy and Evie.

"All my stuff is here." Sienna put her hands on her hips. "So who did this?"

"And why?" added Evie.

Lyra touched the map fragment in her pocket anxiously. Could someone have been looking for it? The only other people who knew about it were Dr Briar and Sam, and Dr Briar wasn't at the school any more. *Sam is, though*, she thought.

"I bet it was the Topaz boys," said Sienna, picking a hoodie up from the floor. "They must have realised we'd been in their dorm yesterday and decided to get their own back."

"But why make such a mess?" said Ivy, looking around. "We didn't wreck their room."

"Maybe they thought it was funny," said Sienna.

"No, they're not that mean," said Evie.

"It could have been Sam, not all the boys," said Lyra. "If Dr Briar didn't tell us the truth, and the map is valuable, then she might have asked Sam to try to find it."

"But she said it wasn't worth anything. Why would she lie?" asked Evie.

"Maybe because it's *really* valuable. So valuable she didn't want us to realise what we had," said Lyra.

Her friends didn't look convinced.

Sienna shook her head. "I still think it was the boys just trying to annoy us."

"We don't know that," Lyra insisted. "We must find the rest of the map quickly in case Dr Briar is looking for it too. Let's go tomorrow morning when everyone else is doing the treasure hunt."

"But we already missed the crossnet match and I want to do treasure hunt!" protested Sienna.

"Me too," said Evie. "Ms Rivers said it would

help us to learn more about the school."

"Tomorrow's our last chance to sneak off without the teachers realising. If we don't go then, we'll have to wait until the weekend," Lyra said impatiently.

"The map can wait," said Sienna, shrugging.

Evie nodded. "I agree with Sienna."

"And me," said Ivy.

"Three votes to one," Sienna told Lyra.

Lyra stared at them. She couldn't believe they would rather take part in the fake treasure hunt than look for the map and some genuine treasure. But the others had voted against her. Feeling very frustrated, she tidied away her things, shoving her clothes into her drawers and yanking the covers straight on her bed.

She was still feeling fed up when it was time to go and settle the unicorns for the night. She made an excuse so the others would go on to the

stables without her and then she stomped after them alone.

Misty whinnied when she saw her. "I thought you weren't coming."

"Sorry," muttered Lyra grumpily, emptying a bucket of sky berries into her manger.

Misty nuzzled her. "Are you OK?"

"Mmm," said Lyra.

"Is this about you wanting to miss the treasure hunt to go and look for the map?" Misty asked. "I heard Sienna telling Sparkle about it."

"The map fragment must be important for Sam to go through our things," said Lyra. "There's no time to lose. We should continue our search tomorrow." On impulse she added, "I think I'll go on my own. Will you come with me?"

Misty looked alarmed. "But what if the teachers find out and we get into trouble?"

Lyra shrugged. "Hopefully they won't."

"Lyra, I don't think you should do this."

Lyra felt a sharp stab of frustration. "Oh, Misty!" she snapped. "Why do you always have to be so boring?"

Misty's eyes widened with hurt and Lyra instantly felt awful. She'd spoken sharply because she was cross and it was no excuse. "Sorry, I didn't mean it," she said quickly as Misty hung her head.

"I really didn't," said Lyra, but Misty just continued to stare at the floor.

Just then, Evie looked over the door. "There

you are, Lyra. Are you coming? We need to get back before the bedtime bell."

Lyra hesitated. She didn't want to leave Misty when she'd hurt her feelings but the teachers were very strict about everyone being back in their dorm on time. She gave Misty a quick hug. "Goodnight," she said, but Misty didn't reply.

Lyra walked back to the dorm feeling very guilty. She shouldn't have snapped at Misty. She was fed up but it wasn't fair to take it out on her sweet-natured unicorn.

"Are you OK?" Evie asked as they got into their pyjamas. "You've been really quiet this evening."

"I've got a headache," Lyra lied.

As she pulled the soft, feather-filled duvet over her head, remorse was coursing through her. *I'll make it up to Misty first thing in the morning*, she promised herself.

# CHAPTER EIGHT

The others quickly fell asleep but Lyra tossed and turned, her thoughts jumping about between Misty and the treasure map. The night felt like it was going on forever. At five o'clock she sat up and looked through the window at the stars twinkling in the frosty sky. A full moon was shining down. *I can't stay in bed any longer*, she thought. *I've got to see Misty and say I'm sorry.* She quietly pulled on her jodhpurs and hoodie and crept out of the dorm.

The early-morning air was icy-cold and her breath froze in white clouds as she ran across the grass towards the stables. As she got closer,

she paused. A unicorn with a long purple and green mane was creeping through the stable yard.

"Misty!" Lyra exclaimed. "Where are you going?"

Misty jumped guiltily. "Lyra!"

"What's going on?" Lyra ran over, her feet crunching on the grass.

Misty hung her head and mumbled, "I … I'm going home."

"Going home?" Lyra stared at her. "What do you mean?"

Misty gulped. "I'm missing my family and, well … I think you'd be happier if you were paired with another unicorn. Someone brave and adventurous, like you."

Lyra stared at her. "But I don't want any other unicorn. I want you. You're perfect for me."

# Lyra and Misty

Misty shook her head. "I'm not. I'm boring."
She heaved a sigh. "Don't try to stop me, Lyra. It's
best if I just go home."

Lyra planted herself in front of her unicorn.
"Stop right there. You're not going anywhere,
Misty," she said forcefully. "I don't want another

unicorn and I'm really sorry about what I said yesterday. It was stupid of me. I was angry and I took it out on you, and that was wrong. You're not boring. You're brilliant and I love you!"

Misty looked at her through her long eyelashes. "Really?" she said tentatively.

"Really," Lyra told her. She put her arms round Misty's neck. "Please will you stay?"

Misty rested her face against Lyra's chest and gave a deep, happy sigh. "Yes," she breathed.

Lyra felt a rush of relief. "Thank you. I really couldn't bear it if you left. I'm so sorry you're feeling homesick." She stroked Misty's silky mane. "You told me you were missing your family and I should have listened. Is there anything I can do to help?"

"Just knowing you want me to stay helps," said Misty softly. "I do miss my family but I won't miss them quite so much now I'm sure that you really want me to be your unicorn."

"I really do, and anytime you want to talk about your family, I promise I'll listen," said Lyra. She kissed Misty's forehead. "I can't wait to meet them. And for you to meet my family too."

They stood there for a long moment until Lyra realised that her toes and fingers were turning to ice. "We'd better go inside. It's freezing out here."

They walked back to the stables, Lyra's arm over Misty's neck.

Misty glanced at the still dark sky. "Why are you up so early?" she asked.

"I couldn't sleep. I was thinking about you and wanting to say sorry and also thinking about the treasure map. I have to search those caves again in case we missed something but the others want to wait until the weekend." Lyra sighed. "I know it's only a few more days but yesterday our dorm was ransacked and I'm worried that someone else is also after the map."

Misty stopped. "Then let's go now."

Lyra frowned. "What?"

"To the caves. You and me," said Misty, nuzzling her. "If you really want to go back there, then I'll come with you."

"Really? Let's do it then! If we're quick, we might even be able to get back in time for the treasure hunt. I'll need to get my explorer's bag first, though; you know, the one with all my useful stuff like torches, a compass, supplies—"

"Go and get it," Misty interrupted. "Hurry!"

A smile lit up Lyra's face. "Misty, you're the best!" Lyra hugged her then raced back to the school.

Sienna, Evie and Ivy were still fast asleep as Lyra tiptoed in and took her rucksack from under her bed. But Evie, in the bed next to her, stirred as she picked it up.

"Lyra?"

Lyra froze.

Sleepily Evie propped herself up, blinking at Lyra through the dark. "What are you doing?"

"Nothing," Lyra whispered. "Go back to sleep."

Evie nodded and curled up under her duvet again.

With her heart beating at double speed, Lyra crept out of the dorm.

She raced across the grass to where Misty was waiting. "Got it!" she whispered, holding up her bag. She vaulted on to Misty's back. "Let's go!"

# CHAPTER NINE

Lyra and Misty had just reached the entrance to the tunnel in the rose garden when they heard the sound of hooves. Lyra swung round and saw the rest of Ruby dorm galloping across the moonlit grass towards them.

"There they are!"

"Lyra! Misty! Wait!"

Sienna and Sparkle reached them first. "What are you doing?" Sienna demanded as Sparkle skidded to a halt.

"I was about to go back to sleep when I realised you were fully dressed and that you had your

explorer's bag," said Evie, catching up, "so I woke the others."

"We went to the stables and saw that Misty was gone," Sienna continued. "Then we spotted some hoofprints on the frosty grass so we followed them."

"And now we've found you!" finished Ivy. "You were about to go hunting for the map without us, weren't you?"

Sienna grinned. "Well, it doesn't matter because now we're coming along too. An early-morning adventure, how awesome is that?"

Lyra felt her heart lift. "Very awesome!" she said, grinning back. "But first we need to be prepared." She rummaged around in her bag and handed out torches. "OK, everyone ready?" They all nodded. "Then follow me!"

Lyra and Misty led the way carefully into the tunnel, crossing the uneven ground until they

reached the end and came out into the cavern where the sparkling river disappeared through the rocky wall.

"We didn't find the map in this tunnel, so it must be in that one!" said Sienna, pointing to the smaller tunnel that they hadn't taken.

"Are you sure? It doesn't have a picture of Daybreak either," Lyra pointed out. "I think we should go back to the last carving we found."

"Lyra's right," said Misty. "If the pictures have led us this far, it doesn't seem right that they suddenly disappear. Let's go back to the last one and have another look around."

Lyra felt a rush of gratitude to Misty for backing her up. She stroked her neck. "Thanks," she whispered as they retraced their steps. Misty snorted happily, and for the first time ever Lyra felt as if they were a real team.

When they got back to the last picture of

Daybreak there was only one way to go. Lyra thought that was odd. All the other carvings had been at tunnel junctions where they had to make decisions. Her mind whirred as she studied it. There was a faint circle surrounding it – identical to the one enclosing the picture on the stair back in their tower.

Holding her breath, Lyra leant down from Misty's back and pressed it hard. Would it work?

The carving moved under her fingers, followed by a loud grating noise. Everyone cried out as a section of the rocky wall at the end of the cavern slid to the side. Through the gap they could see the river widening out and flowing on through more caves.

"That must be where we have to go!" cried Lyra. "Remember the clue: *Find Daybreak, move stone, follow river deep!*"

Evie nodded. "*Find Daybreak, move stone* must

have meant pressing the button."

"So now we follow the deep river," said Lyra.

Misty trotted to the gap. From there Lyra saw that the river had a wide bank on both sides and that there was a large wooden raft tied to a rock, which was bobbing gently on the moving water. "A raft! Let's use it to float down the river."

"Awesome!" said Sienna.

They all clambered through the opening. "Oh, wow, I've never been on a raft before," said Evie, sliding off Sunshine and scrambling across the bank towards the rafts. She reached out to pull it closer but as she did so she overbalanced, toppling into the water with a splash. She yelled and thrashed about as the current started to carry her down the river. Sunshine whinnied in alarm and raced to the water.

"Evie!" Sienna yelled, jumping off Sparkle. She ran to the edge of the bank and reached out

her hand. "Evie, grab hold!"

Lyra leapt off Misty too and also raced over, holding her hand out as well. If they could just grab Evie as she came past…

"Be careful, Lyra!" Misty whinnied shrilly, stamping her hooves in agitation. Purple sparks suddenly swirled into the air along with the sweet smell of burnt sugar. Glancing round, Lyra saw Misty surrounded by a swirl

of iridescent purple bubbles. One bubble swelled as it floated towards the river, shimmering as it grew. It landed on the water, where it seemed to dissolve then reform around Evie.

# Lyra and Misty

Lyra watched in amazement as the bubble carried Evie safely to dry land and then burst, sending thousands of tiny shiny bubbles spinning away overhead.

"Wh-what just happened?" Lyra stammered as Sunshine started nuzzling Evie.

"Misty's found her magic, you doughnut! What do you think just happened?" cried Sienna, thumping her on the back.

"Oh, well done, Misty!" cried Ivy, and all the unicorns whinnied in delight.

"Th-thank you, Misty!" stammered Evie, her teeth chattering. She was soaked and it was cold in the caverns. "I'm so sorry, everyone!"

Lyra stared at Misty in awe. "You got your magic."

"Bubble magic just like my mum," said Misty, looking delighted. "It means that I can protect things, make objects float in the air or even make

bubble bridges. There's all sorts I'll be able to do once I've learnt to control it," she added.

"It's brilliant magic!" said Ivy.

Lyra threw her arms round Misty's neck, happiness shooting through her. Misty had found her magic!

"Three cheers for Misty," said Sienna generously. "You found your magic at just the right time."

"Yes, thanks again, Misty," said Evie.

"We'd better go back and get you dried off," said Ivy, taking in Evie's dripping clothes and chattering teeth.

"But what about the map?" Lyra said. "We've come this far. We can't go back now."

"Evie will catch a chill if she stays in her wet clothes," said Sunshine, breathing warm air on Evie's face.

Lyra felt bad. She didn't want to make Evie ill

but they were so close to discovering the next clue. Suddenly she had an idea. Rummaging in her rucksack, she pulled out a shiny silver blanket and handed it to Evie. "Here, put this round you. It's a survival blanket. It's really light but it will keep you warm. I've also got spare gloves, socks and a hoodie too," she said, digging them out. "But if you still want to go back to school, then that's fine."

Evie pulled the clothes on and wrapped the blanket round her, snuggling down inside it. "I want to go on," she said bravely.

"Really? That's brilliant. Everyone on to the raft then!" Lyra declared.

"What about us?" said Misty. She looked doubtfully at her hooves. "I don't think unicorns and rafts mix."

"We can't leave you behind," said Lyra.

Misty snorted and tossed her mane – finding her magic seemed to have given her new confidence.

"Of course not, and we wouldn't let you go on without us. How about we pull the raft? It's got two ropes. If we pair up and hold on to the ropes, then if the current gets too strong, we can stop the raft going too fast."

Lyra nodded. "Good plan. Let's go."

Misty and Flame held the front rope in their mouths while Sunshine and Sparkle held the back one. There were paddles on the raft; Lyra and Sienna sat near the edges dipping them into the water and the unicorns helped to pull them along. At times the rocky roof soared high above them while sometimes it was so low they had to duck. Lyra's eyes darted everywhere as they floated past. The second piece of the map had to be hidden here somewhere, but where? The clue said it was behind a glittering wall. She scanned the rocky sides of the caverns, but none of them glittered.

# Lyra and Misty

After they'd been travelling for a while, Misty turned to Lyra. "The river's starting to flow faster now," she said, looking anxious. "And I can hear something strange in the distance, a thundering sound. Maybe you should get off the raft?"

"No way!" said Lyra. She'd also noticed the current was getting stronger. The raft was bobbing up and down more and she could see that the unicorns were struggling to hold on to it. But they couldn't give up. They had to find the glittering wall. She looked at the others. "Does anyone else want to get off?"

Sienna shook her head emphatically. "Nope."

"Not yet," said Ivy and Evie.

Lyra grinned at her friends. "That's settled then. Let's carry on."

Misty's face tightened with worry.

"This is awesome!" called Sienna, blinking in the spray as the river started to flow even faster

and the front of the raft began to jump and dip in the water.

Evie gasped and hung on tightly. "It's getting very bouncy!"

"Lyra, I really think we should turn back now!" Misty had to shout to make herself heard over the rushing river.

"Not yet!" Water ran down Lyra's hair and face.

Evie and Ivy squealed as the front of the raft lifted out of the water then crashed back down.

The raft went round a bend in the river and it was then that Lyra saw something that made her heart skip a beat. In front of them was a waterfall.

"We need to get off the raft!" she shrieked. "Everyone paddle to the bank. NOW!"

The unicorns snorted and pulled at the ropes with all their might, their hooves slipping on the wet rock. But the current was too strong. The ropes were wrenched from the unicorns' mouths

and suddenly the girls found themselves adrift, the raft speeding straight towards the top of the waterfall.

*We're going to drown if we go over it*, thought Lyra in terror as she clung on to the raft. *I should have listened to Misty and turned back when she said!*

Her friends were shouting and screaming. The unicorns were all whinnying desperately. But there was no stopping the raft. It accelerated and shot over the edge of the waterfall.

*This is it*, Lyra thought, shutting her eyes as she started to fall.

# CHAPTER TEN

Lyra tumbled through the air surrounded by the roar of the water, but all of a sudden the noise faded. She blinked as she realised she wasn't falling but floating. Floating! A shimmering wall curved all around her. *Misty's bubble magic!*

Lyra leapt to her feet and gazed through the bubble that was carrying her safely down the waterfall. Relief rushed through her as she saw that her friends were also in giant bubbles.

They landed at the bottom and the bubbles bounced them lightly over the surface of the raging river, coming to rest on the banks. Sparkle,

Sunshine and Flame came galloping down the steep path at the side of the waterfall. Misty followed far more slowly, her sides heaving.

Lyra scrambled to her feet. Her legs felt wobbly but she ran up the steep path beside the waterfall, desperate to reach Misty, who was stumbling with exhaustion.

"Misty! You saved us all! I'm so sorry that I didn't listen to you. Are you OK?"

"Yes. Just … just tired," Misty panted. "That took a lot of magic."

"I've got some sky berries," said Lyra, pulling some out of her rucksack that was still on her back. "Here." She fed them to Misty, stroking her all the while.

Misty started to look better. "Sky berries were

just what I needed. You always think of everything," she said.

"Except danger," said Lyra ruefully. "Oh, Misty, I'm so sorry. I promise I'll listen to you more in the future and I'll try not to get us into such dangerous situations."

Misty nuzzled her. "But getting into dangerous situations isn't all bad. If you'd listened to me yesterday and we hadn't come into these caves, I might never have found my magic. And actually, now I know you're all safe, I have kind of enjoyed this adventure."

They hugged until Ivy's yell broke them up. "Lyra, look at your hair!" She was pointing at them from further down the path. "You've bonded!"

Misty picked up a strand of Lyra's long hair with her muzzle. It had turned the same purple and spring green as her mane. "We really have!" she said, nuzzling Lyra. "It's official. We're best friends

forever!"

"And partners in adventure?" Lyra said hopefully.

"And partners in adventure!" Misty echoed happily.

Everyone hurried up the path to join them and gathered round, congratulating them. Beside them the waterfall fell in a thundering sheet of sparkling water and spray.

"I guess we're going to have to walk home," said Sienna, looking at the wrecked raft floating away down the river.

"And we didn't find the map," said Ivy sadly.

"The glittering wall must be further down the river," said Evie.

"Unless…" Lyra pointed to the waterfall. "A glittering wall! Don't you see? That's what the waterfall is. Could the map be hidden behind it?"

They all stared at the sheet of water cascading

down. It did look like a wall. From where they were standing, they could just make out a space behind it and a narrow rocky ledge.

"Do you think the map fragment might be somewhere along that ledge?" Evie asked.

"Yes!" cried Sienna, who had gone closer to the waterfall. She motioned towards a boulder at the edge of the path. "There's a carving of Daybreak here and an arrow pointing towards it."

"I bet it's there," said Lyra. "I'm going to look." She glanced at Misty, wondering if she would try to stop her, but Misty just nodded.

"I'll protect you if you slip," she said.

Lyra felt a warm glow. She trusted Misty completely.

"I'll come too," said Sienna quickly.

"And me!" said both Ivy and Evie.

Misty shook her head. "No, please don't. I'm too tired to save all of you if anything goes wrong."

"I'll be fine. Let me go alone," said Lyra.

Her friends didn't look happy but reluctantly gave in.

"OK, but be careful," Sienna said.

"I will," promised Lyra.

Dropping to her hands and knees, she edged out on to the ledge. The water thundered down in front of her, the spray soaking her all over again. The ledge was wet and slippery and Lyra's heart

raced as she inched along it. It grew even narrower but she could see a small cave just ahead; she was sure that was where she needed to go. She gritted her teeth and kept going until she reached the entrance and crawled inside.

Getting to her feet, she stood up. Her legs were shaky and she was breathing hard. With her back to the cascading water, she shone her torch around the cave. There was nothing there except for a pile of boulders heaped up at the back.

Lyra went over to examine them. A perfectly round boulder was balanced on the top. It had an egg-shaped hole in the middle. Lyra poked a finger inside and heard the crackle of paper. Yes! Her heart turned somersaults as she teased the paper out and carefully unrolled it.

It was the second piece of the map! There was a picture of Daybreak, the crying unicorn, in the top right corner, the rest of the school in the

top left, some more of the maze in the bottom left corner, and in the bottom right corner were drawings of some strange stones. Turning it over, Lyra saw a new riddle to solve.

She rolled the paper up and tucked it inside her hoodie. They could work it out later. Right now she needed to get back to safety.

Lyra crawled carefully back along the ledge. "I found it!" she gasped as she reached the path, and her friends pulled her to safety. "We've got the second piece!"

Misty's eyes shone as everyone whooped and cheered.

Evie looked thoughtful. "The treasure must be really valuable for someone to go to such lengths to hide the map."

"We can't tell anyone else," said Sienna.

Lyra nodded. "Let's all promise to keep it our secret."

"I promise!" everyone chorused.

"Should we take the new piece of map back to our dorm and look at it properly there?" suggested Lyra. "We don't want it to get wet or fall into the river."

"Agreed," said Sienna as she vaulted on to Sparkle. "Come on!"

Lyra was too excited to mind as Sienna and Sparkle took the lead again. She couldn't wait to examine the map properly and work out the next clue.

They got back in the stable yard just as Sam, Nawaz, Archie and Reuben arrived to get their unicorns ready for the treasure hunt.

Sam was carrying two huge bags of warm pastries. He stared at the girls intently. "You're up even earlier than us. Did you skip breakfast to get a head start on the treasure hunt?"

Lyra shook her head. "We just wanted to take our unicorns for a walk – the gardens are so beautiful." She met Sam's eye, hoping that he'd believe her.

Reuben grinned. "I didn't realise you girls were into nature. I love going for early-morning walks on my grandparents' farm."

Sam held out one of the bags of pastries. "We got these from the kitchen for our breakfast but there's plenty to go round," he said gruffly. "Go on, you can have some, seeing as we're dorm neighbours. You must be hungry after your early start."

The other boys nodded.

"Wow! Thanks," the girls said in unison.

Lyra's eyes met Sam's and he smiled. She smiled back, thinking that she couldn't work him out at all. Just when she was convinced he was their enemy and wanted the map for his aunt, he did something really nice like this.

"See you on the treasure hunt," said Reuben as

the girls took a warm pastry each.

Sam gave Lyra a look that was hard to read. "Be prepared to lose! We're going to beat you to the treasure today!" he said.

"You bet we are!" said Archie. "First place is as good as ours!"

The boys high-fived each other then disappeared inside the stable block to find their unicorns.

"We need to get ready," said Sienna, casting a look after the boys.

"I'm tired," Sparkle said.

"Me too," said Misty.

"We could always have breakfast and a rest first," said Ivy.

"But then the boys will have a head start," argued Sienna. "And all the others too." She pointed to more students who were hurrying to the stables.

"So what if they do?" said Lyra. "As soon as we find the rest of the map, we'll have a real treasure

hunt to go on. That's got to be better than a pretend treasure hunt!" She nudged Sienna. "Come on, you know I'm right."

A grin spread across Sienna's face. "OK, I guess you are. Breakfast it is!"

They fetched buckets of sky berries for the unicorns and then sneaked to a quiet spot at the back of the stables and sat down to have their mini feast. The pastries were fresh and crisp, with gooey fillings and drizzles of white icing.

"Yum!" Lyra smiled as she finished her pastry. Licking crumbs from her fingers, she went over to hug Misty, who was grazing nearby. "Oh, Misty, last night I was so unhappy and now I'm happier than I've ever been."

Misty nuzzled her. "Me too. Look at my magic!" She stamped her hoof, showering Lyra in purple sparkles. A stream of glittering multicoloured bubbles rose up around them. "Isn't it cool?"

# Lyra and Misty

"It's brilliant," Lyra said, feeling like she might burst with delight. Now that she was sure that she and Misty would graduate at the end of the year, she could relax and enjoy all the adventures that Unicorn Academy had to offer. She couldn't wait to find the next piece of the map. "I love being here with you," she said, and she sighed happily.

Misty stamped her hoof and the bubbles burst into a rainbow of fireworks. "It really is magic!" she whinnied.

# PRINCESS of PETS

Animal adventures, friendship and a royal family! From the author of The Rescue Princesses.

# Another MAGICAL series from Nosy Crow!

## SNOW SISTERS